ashlee simpson

Ashlee Simpson has it all—a number-one album, a hit reality show, and awards and accolades from both peers and critics. (Not to mention a famous big sister!)

But before she became a chart-topping rocker, Ashlee had to figure out a way to introduce herself as someone other than "Jessica's little sister" and prove to the world that she had what it takes to be a superstar. And she sure did! America's favorite little sister has grown into a full-fledged rock star and has attracted thousands of fans with her down-to-earth attitude and honest songwriting.

With her brown hair, beat-up sneakers, and individual style, Ashlee Simpson has definitely emerged from the shadow and into the spotlight!

ashlee simpson

Out of the Shadow and into the Spotlight

by Grace Norwich

Simon Spotlight
New York London Toronto Sydney

SIMON SPOTLIGHT
An imprint of Simon & Schuster Children's Publishing Division
1230 Avenue of the Americas, New York, New York 10020

Designed by Chani Yammer
The text of this book is set in Centaur.

Manufactured in the United States of America
First Edition 10 9 8 7 6 5 4 3 2 1

Library of Congress Catalog Card Number 2004114312
ISBN 1-4169-0395-X

Contents

1

Out from Her Sister's Shadow

Ashlee Simpson has a lot in common with her older sister, Jessica. Both girls obviously come from the same tight-knit, loving family. They both grew up in Texas, and they both like to return whenever they can. That's normal. But this isn't your typical pair of sisters. Ashlee and Jessica both have amazing voices and extremely successful careers in the music industry. And as if that weren't enough, each sister has also starred in her own hit reality show on MTV. *Newlyweds: Nick & Jessica* allowed viewers to watch Jessica settle into married life with her husband, the adorable Nick Lachey, while *The Ashlee Simpson Show* followed Ashlee through every step of making her first album. Basically, the Simpson sisters both lead all-around spectacular lives marked by a winning combination of ambition and talent.

Despite their similarities—some common and some not so common—deep down Ashlee and Jessica couldn't be more different. Jessica is the picture-perfect image of every school's most popular cheerleader. She's the overall good girl with gorgeous long blond hair, a perfect smile, and a giggly, fun-loving personality. Jessica's the kind of girl others might be jealous of because she's so perfect, but they can't really resent her because she's just too nice. She even got her start in music by attending church!

Jessica first discovered her remarkable vocal talent while singing gospel songs in the Baptist church where her father, Joe Simpson, was the minister. When she hit the big time as a pop star, belting out soulful R&B tunes, Jessica shed her pure image and wore outfits that were every bit as outrageous and revealing as performers almost twice her age. But despite the short skirts and low tops, the older Simpson sister remained a traditional girl through and through, and she was proud to use her fame to be a good role model for her younger fans.

While Jessica is the golden girl who favors pink Ugg boots and Juicy Couture sweat suits, Ashlee is the quirky chick who feels more comfortable in a pair of beat-up sneakers, loose-fitting jeans, and a ripped tank top. In terms of style, Ashlee is definitely the rebel of the Simpson clan. Her sister's music is in the genre of such divas as Whitney Houston, but Ashlee's is more in the tradition of tough rock-'n'-roll women such as The Pretenders' Chrissie Hynde and Blondie's Debbie Harry. "Jessica and I are like night and day," Ashlee explained to *Entertainment Weekly*. "She grew up listening to Celine Dion and Mariah Carey. I grew up listening to Alanis Morissette and Green Day."

The first album Ashlee ever bought was Alanis's hit debut CD, the unmistakably edgy *Jagged Little Pill*. Already the little rebel at eleven years old, Ashlee went out and purchased it without asking her parents' permission. Her mom, Tina, wasn't too happy when she heard the album had curse words in the lyrics, so when Ashlee's friends bought tickets to Morissette's concert, her mom wouldn't let her go. Little Ashlee was so mad that she swore at her mother with the same curse words she had learned while listening to Alanis's record. Ashlee quickly realized who was boss in the Simpson home when, as she told *YM*, "My mom washed my mouth out with soap."

But it's not just Ashlee's dyed, dramatic dark hair and funky musical taste that separate her from her blond sister. The two have been like opposite sides of the same coin ever since they were little girls living in Texas. In the fifth grade Ashlee was obsessed with the band Green Day and attended punk shows where she would throw herself into the mosh pit. While this tiny blond girl was enjoying banging up against a bunch of big punks, Jessica was voted homecoming queen of her high school two years in a row. "Jessica's always been the quiet, conservative one," Ashlee told *Blender* magazine. "Me, I'm the artsy one, the girl in the tutu and the Converse sneakers, the girl with knots in her hair."

That difference was sometimes hard on Ashlee while she was growing up. Around her pretty, well-adjusted sister, she felt like an outsider. Can you believe this gorgeous girl ever felt like an outcast? The truth is, she did. Especially when her popular sister had friends come over to the house. Feeling left out of the fun, Ashlee, not yet a teenager, showed a defiant side that would later play a part in her music. She ran downstairs, in only a bathrobe, to where her sister was hanging out with all her cool friends. In order to get some attention, Ashlee took off the robe and played the guitar naked in front of everybody! Jessica nearly died of embarrassment. "The more Jessica begged me to stop, the more I tried to annoy her," Ashlee said in *Blender* magazine. "I was just, you know, having fun. I've always been kind of flamboyant."

Anyone who is a little sister knows how hard it can be to compete with an older sibling. They always seem smarter, better, bigger. Just imagine what it must have been like to have *Jessica Simpson* as an older sister! As Jessica became more and more famous, young Ashlee felt smaller and smaller. Being in Jessica's shadow really got to her at times (later, when she'd grown out of her jealousy, Ashlee wrote a song about this for her first album).

Soon enough Ashlee overcame her insecurities, realizing that she wasn't more awkward or any less cool than her sister. She tried her hand at acting and landed small roles on TV and the big screen until she scored a reoccurring part as Cecilia Smith on the popular WB show *7th Heaven*. Ashlee found her own place in the spotlight, but she still couldn't escape her sister's presence. Journalists and fans were constantly asking her how she thought she measured up to Jessica. For Ashlee, the endless comparisons were frustrating for many reasons. "People run up to [Jessica] to tell her what a great role model she is," Ashlee told *YM*. "I agree—Jessica's the best—but that's a lot for me to live up to." Ashlee wanted to become her own person and her own star.

Although she has always been interested in pursuing a career as a recording artist, Ashlee definitely didn't want to appear as if she were just the little sister tagging along after her older sister. So she was hesitant to dive into the music business. However, it seemed almost inevitable that she would eventually follow in Jessica's footsteps. The two have always been extremely close and share so much with each other—including talent!

Today Ashlee is proving that you don't have to be perfect, blond, or an older sister to be a big success. Prior to her record release she gained millions of fans by demonstrating a carefree, fun-loving attitude on her reality TV show, and the end result was unimaginable. With the 2004 release of her debut album, *Autobiography,* an edgy, soulful collection of songs that reveal her intimate emotions on a range of life experiences, Ashlee exploded onto the music scene as an international superstar. Her face is on the cover of national magazines, and gossip columns track what parties she goes to and speculate about her love life. Ashlee's album sold four hundred thousand copies in its first week—a record even her own sister has never achieved! As for Jessica, she is taking a few notes from her little sister. "It's different now because I'm actually becoming successful and it had nothing to do with her," Ashlee told the *Monterey County Herald.* "Jessica and I have actually switched because she wants to go into acting. Now she comes to me for advice."

Jessica had better listen up. Her little sister's offbeat individuality is gaining a lot of attention. Ashlee is lucky because she knows her put-together sister always has her back, but this raven-haired wild child is now telling the world, "I have my own identity and I stand on my own," as she said in *USA Today.*

2

Deep in the Heart of Texas

Ashlee Simpson was born in Dallas, Texas, on October 3, 1984, to her mother, Tina, an aerobics instructor, and her father, Joe, a youth minister and adolescent therapist who specialized in working with abused children. Being the little sister had its benefits. While Jessica, who is four years older than Ashlee, was for the most part a goody-goody, first born children always wear down even the strictest of parents. "It was easier on me because Jessica broke in our parents," Ashlee said to the *New York Post*. This was definitely a good thing since

Ashlee wasn't exactly the best rule follower. "I think I was harder to handle than Jess. When my parents told me to do something, I'd always try to do the opposite."

A huge part of growing up in the Simpson household was church. It's pretty hard to get out of Sunday morning services when your dad is the minister. But faith isn't just a weekend thing with the Simpson clan. It infuses almost everything they do. Still, as a child Ashlee found her own little ways to rebel, even when it came to her dad's services. Ashlee was about six years old when she decided she wasn't going to be any ordinary member of her family's Baptist congregation. One Sunday she marched right into the church barefoot! She didn't stop at the door, but instead went right up to the pulpit where her father used to preach and decided to shock everyone by pulling her skirt over her head and turning around very slowly. Needless to say, the congregation thought that was a pretty strange thing to do, especially for a preacher's daughter.

This behavior was very different from that of her gospel-singing sister, Jessica, who developed her singing talent at church, while Ashlee chose to flash the congregants. Jessica was already in the choir at the age of five, and only a few years later she became a soloist. Everyone quickly recognized the emotional power of Jessica's voice when she performed "Amazing Grace" and other gospel songs, and they knew they were in the presence of real talent.

At the age of twelve Jessica auditioned for *The New Mickey Mouse Club*, where many of today's pop stars, such as Justin Timberlake, Britney Spears, and Christina Aguilera got their start. Responding to a nationwide casting call that drew more than thirty thousand girls from around the country, Jessica was one of a few who were chosen to go on to the final round of auditions to become a Mouseketeer. But it would be a bit longer before she made her break into the music business. Although she made it all the way to the final auditions, in the end, as she told *Business Wire*, "I just froze." The problem was that her audition came right after the amazing Christina Aguilera's performance. Jessica sat in the green room (the place where performers wait before going onstage) listening to the grown-up voice of the future superstar come out of tiny Christina. Faced with following that act, Jessica lost her nerve. But even though she had felt intimidated at *The New Mickey Mouse Club* trials and was bitterly disappointed at not landing a spot, Jessica knew she still wanted to pursue singing.

She kept performing at church events, where she felt more comfortable. At age thirteen Jessica sang at her church camp, where a man who had started a gospel record label heard her voice and soon after started working with her on her first record. Unfortunately Jessica would again have to wait for success, since the record label went out of business a week before her album was finished. She kept at it, though, taking her music on the road (her grandmother kicked in seventy-five hundred dollars to have the disc completed) and traveling with her father to Christian youth conferences where she sang, wearing costumes made by her mom, for as many as twenty thousand people at once. "Everywhere my dad would speak," Jessica told *Business Wire,* "I would perform." They ended up selling every record that her grandma had paid for. Finally Jessica did branch out of the Christian music scene (although she remains religious to this day) and hit the big time when in 1997 Tommy Mottola, who was then the Sony Music Entertainment chairman and CEO, heard her sing in his office. "I was so nervous, you know, because he listens to Mariah [Carey] all the time," Jessica told the *Fort Worth Star-Telegram.* This time she didn't buckle under the pressure like she had at *The New Mickey Mouse Club* audition. Instead she nailed her performance and began her ascent to the top of the music charts. Or, as Jessica put it, "I sang for him and he signed me on the spot."

Ashlee has also always loved to perform, but in a *very* different way from her sister. How else to explain her childhood exhibitionism at church? People constantly misinterpreted her intentions when she acted out. Just because she was a little bit offbeat and did wild things for the fun of doing something different didn't mean that her heart wasn't in the same place as Jessica's when she nailed those five-octave-range songs. "I'm not the evil sister. I'm the sister who's a little more out there," Ashlee told the *New York Post.* "If there's something I want to try, I'm going to do it. People confuse edgy and bad, but I'm not, like, scary or anything. I just step close to the line."

The Simpsons are a very musical family, and a passion for singing seems to be part of their genetic makeup. The sisters' grandma (Tina's mom) plays the violin and piano, and Tina herself has a great voice, which of course she passed along to her daughters. When they can take a little time out of their hectic schedules and hang out as a family, Ashlee, her sister, and her mom love to sit around and sing together. "Me, her, and Jessica sing together all the time," Ashlee told the *New York Times*. "We'll sing, like, gospel songs or, whatever, blues songs." (That is, when they aren't busy enjoying their other favorite pastime—shopping!)

Although she is now a big recording star and talks about singing with her family for fun, as a child Ashlee kept her passion for singing to herself. She could bare her butt to a bunch of churchgoers but she couldn't show her mom and dad that she wanted to rock out. But Ashlee's hesitation to share her dreams is understandable. Punk rock isn't usually parents' top music choice, and that's exactly what little Ashlee loved, not sappy ballads or sugary pop songs. Plus, singing was Jessica's thing. Everyone in church knew it, and once she signed a record contract the whole world would know it too. So Ashlee limited her love of singing to doing Alanis Morissette impressions secretly in her room.

Music would have to wait for Ashlee, but

that didn't mean her only creative outlet was going to be playing air guitar in her bedroom. Not even close. Ashlee found her own way to shine, and that was through dancing. At age three Ashlee began training as a classical ballet dancer, and sure enough, thanks in part to that Simpson drive, she became one of the best young dancers in Texas. It's funny that Ashlee, who liked to throw herself into the mosh pit and rock out in her room, would want to be a part of the strict and serious world of ballet. In order to become a professional, ballet dancers spend hours a day practicing, repeating the same movements in order to get their toes to point perfectly, and to look like they are floating when they leap into the air. It's one of the hardest forms of art to master and takes a huge amount of dedication. Plus the classical music! Green Day couldn't be any more different from *Swan Lake*. But Ashlee loved to dance. It also didn't hurt that Jessica readily admits to having absolutely no dancing ability at all (anyone who has watched her

MTV reality show *Newlyweds* knows what a lovable klutz she is).

Through ballet, the little sister gained a stage of her own. And Ashlee knew how to take advantage of the spotlight. When she was eleven years old, she became the youngest person ever accepted to the School of American Ballet, one of the best ballet schools in the country. Originally founded by dance legends George Balanchine and Lincoln Kirstein, the School of American Ballet is the official training center for the prestigious New York City Ballet. Most students who train at the school go on to become world-class professional dancers or choreographers. Ashlee had to go through an incredibly hard, ultracompetitive auditioning process (think *Save the Last Dance* times a thousand!), but the hardest part of the experience was after she got accepted. The School of American Ballet is located in New York City, so Ashlee had to leave her family in Texas and move by herself all the way to the big city, where she lived in a dorm with other dancers.

For the next two years Ashlee worked hard to pursue her dream of becoming a professional ballet dancer. Meanwhile her big sister was also hard at work pursuing her own dreams and gearing up for her first album, *Sweet Kisses.* Ashlee was presented with a once-in-a-lifetime opportunity to study dancing at the world-famous Kirov Ballet in Russia. But her dad wouldn't let her go. Soon after, the entire Simpson family moved to Los Angeles together so that Jessica could move full steam ahead to pop stardom. Having started dancing at just three years old, Ashlee was extremely disappointed. It looked like the little sister was going to get the short end of the stick again! Luckily, Ashlee didn't need to sulk for too long, since big things were awaiting her in L.A.

3

Big Star, Little Star

In 1999, after two years of frustration over delays and fretting over recording sessions, Jessica's career was finally taking off. Her first single, "I Wanna Love You Forever", was making a big splash. Her heart-wrenching voice, glowing looks, and wholesome personality was a killer combination that set her apart from the growing horde of young stars. Teen magazines such as *Teen* and *Teen People* happily embraced this homecoming queen from Texas and prominently featured her on their pages. Despite her unique story, naturally she was compared to another famous teen blonde,

Britney Spears. This was something that Jessica didn't always appreciate. She bluntly told the *Fort Worth Star-Telegram*, "I am not trying to be her."

One of the biggest elements of having a successful career in music is touring. Famous singers and bands often have to spend most of their year on the road when they have an album out, because if they don't play it to audiences, people will not get excited about their music. Sure, videos and television appearances are important nowadays, but performing live is still the backbone of a musician's career. In a way, it's where the music begins and ends for them. It's also where they get a lot of inspiration and energy. Ashlee, then fourteen, got to experience the excitement of touring firsthand when her sister hit the road to promote her first album.

Jessica was going on her first tour, opening for the hot boy band 98 Degrees, which counted among its members none other than her future husband, Nick Lachey. Of course,

Jessica didn't know that when she first met him. Soon the two began dating—who could blame her for snatching up the cute singer with the sly grin, gigantic muscles, and a band that sold millions of albums? So what if he wouldn't have exactly fit into Jessica's church youth group circle with his tattoos and piercings. This was show biz, right?

Jessica knew that Ashlee had been devastated about not going to Russia to study dance, and she knew her little sister had an incredible talent. "She was runner-up for national junior dancer of the year at New York City Dance Alliance," Jessica bragged to *Business Wire* at the time. "So she's like an amazing dancer." Up to this point Jessica's career had always been a family affair, and it was working out so well, it didn't make sense for her to take a break from music. The solution was a no-brainer; Jessica asked Ashlee if she would join her tour as one of her backup dancers. She would have not only her fun little sister around to keep her company, but also an awesome addition to her concert troupe. "Jessica was like, 'You're as good as or even better than most dancers,'" Ashlee said to *YM.* "It was the most exciting thing for me because I was only fourteen."

This turned out to be an excellent idea, and Ashlee ended up touring with her sister for three years, during which Jessica's album, *Sweet Kisses,* released by Columbia Records, became a big hit and sold two million copies. The singer performed more than sixty shows with 98 Degrees on the Heat It Up tour before she opened for another huge star, Latin cutie Ricky Martin. Mom and Dad were always close by, with Joe as Jessica's manager (a position he would later take on for Ashlee) and Tina working on costumes.

Jessica continued to open for other performers until she finally headlined her own tour while promoting her second album, *Irresistible.* This was a major step for everybody, including Ashlee. The Dreamchaser tour, as it was called, was an amazing show. With the band, the dancers, the costume changes, and a stage wired with 100,000 watts of sound and lights, the act was a huge—and rewarding—challenge every night.

That kind of challenge wasn't always easy, especially for someone as young as Ashlee. "It was fun, sure," Ashlee told *Blender*. "But it was also pretty horrible." At times, some of the other dancers were mean to her because she was, well, the little sister of the big star. Although they gave her a "tough time," Ashlee said that now that she has made a name for herself in music (and is a bit older and wiser), "those same people are calling to congratulate me." Which just goes to prove that the real world can be just like school—full of awkward social situations.

Jessica had a more traditional adolescence than Ashlee did. Jessica attended J.J. Pearce High School in Texas, which she left after her junior year to pursue music full-time. Later on she earned her high school diploma through a correspondence course given by Texas Tech University. But because Ashlee left regular school fairly early in her life to be on the stage, she really got her education on the road. Ashlee had to do her homework in between shows while dancing with her sister on a major musical tour. Studying happened everywhere, including on the tour bus. "When everyone else got to go play, I'd have to sit down and do work in the back of the bus," she told the *New York Times*. "Every class that you go through in high school, my mom taught me. And then my sister's dancers would come over and help me out, if I needed to know something. Jessica had a Latin dancer, so I was going through Spanish class and he would totally help me out." So it turns out, the other dancers weren't all that bad. After all, they helped Ashlee to earn her high school diploma by the time she was sixteen.

With all its ups and downs, touring with her sister and being in the heart of show business really made Ashlee understand something she had always known about herself—that she is a true entertainer. Dancing behind her sister proved to Ashlee that performing was what she wanted to do with her life too. "I've always been the biggest nut!" Ashlee told *Teen People*. "I feel so good onstage. It's like an out-of-body experience."

Although she got her start by backing up her sister, Ashlee realized that she needed to strike out on her own to make her wish come true.

4

Acting Out

While dancing behind her sister onstage, Ashlee had gotten a taste of the bright lights and roaring crowds that went with being a star. She began to look for ways other than dancing to satisfy her creative impulses and put her in the spotlight. She wasn't ready to take the plunge into a musical career of her own. That was still big sis's territory, and it was a smart business decision to keep her distance until she could completely forge her own identity in that arena. (Although, let's face it, sixteen-year-old Ashlee was hardly the picture of a hard-nosed businesswoman!)

So there was only one thing left to try: acting. Ashlee's new home base of L.A. was filled with countless other girls just like herself—pretty, talented, and eager to "make it." Most aspiring actresses in Hollywood struggle for years trying to get bit parts, if they land any parts at all. It's a rough business, even for someone like Ashlee, who had a tough manager father, a supportive mom, and a budding star of a sister. She would face stiff competition for even the smallest of roles. But this is a girl who went to New York alone when she was eleven years old. Ashlee certainly wasn't going to put her goals aside because of a little competition.

While still performing as a backup dancer for Jessica, Ashlee began auditioning for acting gigs. In 2000 Ashlee appeared in an episode of the Emmy award-winning show *Malcolm in the Middle,* a popular sitcom on Fox about Malcolm (played by Frankie Muniz) and his three brothers (Christopher Kennedy Masterson, Justin Berfield, and Erik Per

Sullivan), who are always fighting and trying the patience of their supremely hassled parents (Bryan Cranston and Jane Kaczmarek). Making an appearance on such a great show was wonderful for Ashlee's career, but she still needed a meaty role where she could show directors and fans what she was capable of doing.

In 2001 she landed her first movie role in *The Hot Chick.* Her part was very small, but it was in a major studio film—an opportunity many actresses only dream of getting. *The Hot Chick,* which starred the hilarious comedian Rob Schneider, is a film about a really mean, popular girl in high school (played by Rachel McAdams) who wakes up one day to find she's been turned into a thirty-year-old man. The film brought in $35 million in U.S. ticket sales when it came out—not exactly a blockbuster, but that's still a lot of people who saw Ashlee up on the big screen! While *The Hot Chick* was certainly not going to earn Ashlee any Academy Awards, it did give her acting career another boost. Little did she know, she was about to get her biggest break yet.

In 2002, *7th Heaven,* a television family drama about the life of a sensitive minister, his wife, and their seven children, was the highest-rated series on the WB, a popular network among teens. Created by Brenda Hampton, *7th Heaven* explores many difficult subjects that currently affect young people. The plotlines have touched upon everything from vandalism to violence in schools to the Holocaust. Even though the story centers around Reverend Eric Camden, played by Stephen Collins, and deals a lot with issues of faith, the show doesn't shy away from dealing with real topics, such as teen pregnancy and drug use. Of course there are a lot of light moments, as one might expect with seven kids around, but the serious material is what has helped earn the show awards and honors from organizations like the Parents Television Council and the Academy of Religious Broadcasting (to be fair, the light stuff probably helped *7th Heaven* win its Kids'

Choice and Teen Choice Awards).

7th Heaven has always revolved around the Camden household, but during 2002, the show's seventh season, the writers decided to make the characters of Lucy Kinkirk, one of the Camdens' daughters, played by Beverley Mitchell, and her brother Simon Camden, played by David Gallagher, more important to the show's plotlines. New characters were introduced to make Lucy's and Simon's lives more intriguing. What could be more tantalizing to devoted *7th Heaven* watchers than a pretty new love interest for the absolutely adorable Simon?

Enter Ashlee. The part was perfect for her, since the show deals a lot with the subject of faith and people who are trying to live a Christian life in the modern world. That's an experience very close to Ashlee's heart since she came from a religious family. She could relate to Simon Camden's character because her own dad was a preacher and she had been raised with a lot of the same values that are embraced on the show. (It doesn't hurt that she is also super cute and any guy's dream date, right?) The director and casting agents recognized what an ideal actress Ashlee was for the part, and their decision to cast her as Cecilia Smith turned out to be a good one for everybody, including the show's fans. In the original deal Ashlee was only supposed to be on seven episodes, but the audience responded to her character so well, she wound up appearing on the hit series for two seasons. During her run on *7th Heaven,* fans watched as her character went through many things that normal teens go through, including breakups and problems with parents.

Besides the perks of working with seasoned writers and a cast of top actors on a hit show airing on one of the coolest networks around, Ashlee also got to play Simon's new girlfriend. That meant a lot of serious smooching with her hottie costar David. Their characters even considered having sex at one point during the show, but decided to keep things PG-rated. (Although, in one episode the two of them were kicked out of a movie theater for making out during a G-rated film!) Always a professional on and off the set, Ashlee never complained about her work. "Being Simon's love interest is so fun," Ashlee revealed on the show's Web site. "We made out the first time we met. [David] is a really good kisser. Do you know how many girlfriends he's had on the show? I'm sure he kisses girls all the time." As the character of Cecilia progressed, Ashlee was required to do even more smooching, and not just with Simon. After Simon and Cecilia broke up, she fell into the arms of Tyler Hoechlin's character, Martin Brewer. Can you blame her? Who wouldn't fall for those dark lashes?

When asked during a celebrity MSN online chat session who was a better kisser, Tyler or David, Ashlee graciously replied, "They are both very good kissers and adorable. It's never like a real kiss when you're doing screen kisses. David was my first on-screen kiss." You would think that if you were about to kiss either of these two studs you would get out some serious breath mints and layer on the gloss. But not Ashlee, who tends to prefer to act goofy like one of the guys. So what *does* she do to prepare for an on-screen kiss? "Nothing," Ashlee joked online. "Tyler and I would joke around and eat pickles and Doritos and see who could get the worst breath." Yuck! So much for the glamorous world of TV.

5
Sing it, Sister

Those Simpson girls can't sit still for long.

Jessica had forged a successful music career at last, which had been her goal since she was belting out gospel songs in the church choir. She had also married the man of her dreams when she and Nick tied the knot in October 2002. Still, she decided to take her fame to another level and venture into television. She put her life on view for the entire world to see with *Newlyweds: Nick & Jessica*. The MTV hit turned Jessica into a bigger star than anyone could have expected. Since the show first aired in the summer of 2003, she's been considering movie and television projects, singing for the Indianapolis 500 and the Orange Bowl, appearing in commercials, posing for magazines, and turning out new albums.

Meanwhile, on *7th Heaven*, Ashlee had a role that millions of actresses would kill for. She had gained the admiration of her costars, network executives, and most importantly, fans. But like her sister, Ashlee wasn't satisfied with simply resting on her already incredible achievements. She had to keep pushing herself to go further.

After two seasons on *7th Heaven*, her next step would be bold: She decided to test the waters of the music business—the one thing she had been too timid to try before. Ashlee's first professional singing debut came when she performed the song "Just Let Me Cry" on the soundtrack for the Disney movie *Freaky Friday*, which was released in 2003 and featured Lindsay Lohan and Jamie Lee Curtis as a mother and daughter who switch bodies for a day.

This was a huge step for Ashlee. She obviously had the talent, but she had to conquer her fears. Ashlee readily admits that Jessica was such a good singer, it intimidated her when she was a kid. She felt too shy to sing in front of her family, let alone in public. "I was scared I wouldn't be good enough," Ashlee told *YM*. "So I'd wait till everyone was out of the house, and then I'd go to my room and sing." It's amazing that despite this fear, she found the strength not only to overcome it but also to go on to sing a song for a major motion picture.

With the release of "Just Let Me Cry," Ashlee became a bona fide singer on top of being an actress. Her role as Cecilia was going strong, but she was encouraged by her brief stint as a musician. In fact, Ashlee loved both acting and singing, so it was very hard for her to pick one over the other. But when push came to shove, she had to make a choice. And she chose singing because it gives her a chance to express herself. This was a huge decision. For Ashlee, communicating who she is and what she believes is very important. In the realm of acting, she plays characters, portraying other people as they go through made-up scenarios and pretending to experience their emotions. Baring herself to the public through music appeals to Ashlee, but it also means taking a big risk. "When you act, you're in a role. If they [the viewers] don't like the character you play, it doesn't mean they don't like *you*," she told the *New York Post*. "When you make an album of your own music, you're putting everything on the line."

Singing for *Freaky Friday* was a great kick start to her musical career. It let Ashlee know she could perform in a professional and high-pressure setting. But the song was far from the edgy sound produced by the women in rock whom Ashlee admired. She wasn't looking to become the next Britney Spears, or even the next Jessica Simpson. She had always really admired tough female singers, and as a kid rocking out in her room she had loved the raspy, rough voices of Chrissie Hynde, Pat

Benatar, and Joan Jett. Those were the people who inspired Ashlee as an artist.

Ashlee wanted to rock, and the only way for her to do it was to get started on her very own album, one that would really express all the mixed-up, crazy emotions she and tons of teenage girls just like her feel. In late 2003 she signed a recording contract with Geffen Records and got her big chance. When it came time to work on the record, it was really important to Ashlee to write her own songs. She wanted to make sure her first album truly reflected who she is, including both the good and the bad. "I wasn't going to make a record unless I could write on every song," Ashlee told *Airplay Monitor*. "You can almost tell when someone writes themselves, because there's an honesty that comes out when you're performing. It really makes a difference to speak from your own experiences." While most people freak out if they have to write a term paper, let alone turn their deepest personal feelings into songs for the whole world to hear, Ashlee loved the experience. It wasn't such a stretch for her since she had been writing ever since she was a little girl, long before she knew she'd be making an album (incidentally, keeping a personal journal seems to be a family affair. Jessica has a ritual of writing in her diary every night before she goes to bed). So Ashlee had a trove of material to work with before she even started on her first album, which she aptly titled *Autobiography.*

Ashlee had the raw talent and material, but she did get some much-valued help from a team of seasoned record industry insiders who could show her the ropes, including one of the best pros in the business. John Shanks, who produced and cowrote *Autobiography,* has collaborated with Michelle Branch, Sheryl Crow, and Melissa Etheridge. Those ladies are all great musicians who have had incredible success, but there is one other person John worked with that really impressed Ashlee: Alanis Morissette! Ashlee was working with the very same man who had helped create the music that had inspired her as a little girl (the music that had also led her to get her mouth washed out with soap. Hey, sometimes you gotta suffer for art, right?).

John wasn't the only guy helping out on her record who had good credentials. Writing the songs for her album gave Ashlee a chance to meet a lot of very cool and highly respected people in the music business. Stan Frazier from the band Sugar Ray pitched in his writing skills for the song "Unreachable," which is about the pain love can sometimes bring. "I've been a huge fan of Sugar Ray for a while, so that was cool," Ashlee told MTV.com. The guys from Good Charlotte and John Feldmann from Goldfinger cowrote three other songs with her as well. Ashlee admitted, "It's just fun to collaborate with people that are like, artists, and kind of have a different perspective."

Some adults questioned Ashlee's choice of title for her first album. How could such a young person really have an autobiography?

How many real experiences could happen to a person who's only been alive for nineteen years? But Ashlee *has* been through a lot. "It's where I'm at in my life," she explained on *Good Morning America.* "And, like, a lot of things I have been through, like, you know—Jessica Simpson's sister, *7th Heaven*—I'm like, okay, here's my story. I'm going to tell you who I am."

Ashlee has always proven herself to be a pretty tough chick, so she wasn't going to shy away from the difficult emotions that are a part of growing up and resort to easy, light themes when it came to material for her album. The hard stuff is what makes friendships, relationships, and even albums interesting. "I'm nineteen, and I'm going through some defining moments in my life. I've tried not to hold anything back," she said to *Airplay Monitor.* "I want to step outside of my life and reflect on the things that are happening to me now and write about it. I guess I should apologize to all of the boys that I have used for inspiration." Ashlee's album is full of songs about things that most teenagers can relate to and identify with. And isn't that the point of music? Well, that and having something with a good beat to dance to, and Ashlee delivers on both counts!

The result of all of Ashlee's work and thoughts and musical influences is an album that is much edgier than anything anyone could imagine a sibling of Jessica Simpson producing. *Autobiography* features a lot of guitar, and each song has its own individual message. The title of "Love Me for Me" basically sums up this tune, which is about self-acceptance and persevering in life. The album is filled with soul searching and self-discovery. Of course, a big part of a nineteen-year-old girl's self-defining musical journey includes a lot of talk about boyfriends and all the problems they pose. "Love Makes the World Go Round" tells the story of broken hearts and disappointed dreams, while "Surrender" is about the death of a relationship and growing stronger because of it.

As to the sound of her album, Ashlee certainly didn't want to mimic any specific style she had previously heard, even if she loved it. She wants her sound to be unique. She may admire Chrissie Hynde or Pat Benetar, but Ashlee listens to all kinds of music; her tastes are really broad. She loves bands like Jimmy Eat World, the Pretenders, and Maroon 5, but sometimes when she feels mellow she enjoys a little Bob Marley. "When I went in to make the record I didn't try for a certain sound," she said during an MSN online chat. "I just wanted the music to sound like me and to be an expression of myself."

With the debut of *Autobiography,* Ashlee radically changed her public image from the sweet Cecilia of *7th Heaven* that many people had come to know. Her music brought out the rebellious girl that the Baptist churchgoers of her hometown had gotten a glimpse of early on, but whom few other Americans had seen.

Ashlee reached out to teens by putting her personality into her music, and she hoped to revive the image of the bold rocker babes she admired as a kid. Women like Pat Benetar and Chrissie Hynde, who care more about their lyrics than lip gloss, are a breed of musician Ashlee doesn't think is abundant enough in today's music world. "It's sad because I miss seeing that," she explained to MTV.com. "I love Gwen Stefani. I'm a huge fan of Courtney Love, but I'd like to see a good rocker. But I don't know why there's less women right now. I was probably like eleven years old when I went to Lilith Fair and I saw Jewel and Joan Osborne, and I was like, 'I want to be like them.'" While Ashlee was creating her own album, the role models she looked to were the same ones she had loved as a child, the stars of the eighties. Where were the female idols of the nineties and this decade? "Women need to step up," she told MTV.com.

Having put her heart and soul into her first album, Ashlee was well on the way to "stepping up" on behalf of women her age. *Autobiography* was also a big step toward her ultimate personal goal of introducing the world to the Simpson sister she has always been on the inside. "Finishing my album was amazing. It felt like a journey," she said in an MSN online chat. "When I finished I felt I had grown stronger."

Ashlee had certainly come a long way from being the shy girl obsessed with rock music who sang alone in her room. "I don't hide my singing - not anymore," she told the *7th Heaven* Web site. "I sing punk music actually. I love to run around and scream and rock out and play guitar."

6

Going Solo

A month before her record debuted, Ashlee released her first single, "Pieces of Me," a sassy, flirty tune about her then-boyfriend, fellow musician Ryan Cabrera. A single is like a musician's way of testing the waters before an album comes out. The success of the single often predicts how well the album will eventually be received by the public. From the beginning, Ashlee's single got serious radio play, and fans couldn't wait to hear more.

Ashlee soon embarked on a whirlwind publicity tour to support her new album. Twenty-four hours before the release of

Autobiography on July 20, 2004, she sat for interviews with Regis Philbin and Kelly Ripa, David Letterman, and the holy grail for musicians: *Rolling Stone* magazine. Right before the biggest day of her life, she had to thoughtfully answer questions about herself and be charming on national TV. While she was joking around with David Letterman, she was probably nervously wondering how critics and music fans all across America were going to react to her album the next day.

It turns out, Ashlee didn't have much to worry about. In fact, soon she would have a lot to celebrate. When *Autobiography* hit stores on July 20, it was a huge success. Not only was the media comparing her raspy voice to such legendary rockers as Joan Jett, but also the CDs were flying off the shelves before her record company could replenish the dwindling stock.

Geffen Records's copresident Jordan Schur had a philosophy when he began working with Ashlee. He didn't want Ashlee's history, in terms of her sister's career and her own work on TV, to get in the way of making good music. Jordan believed that Ashlee could make it on her own, without all the other publicity trappings. This was a huge vote of confidence. But his belief that Ashlee's music could stand on its own also meant a lot of work for her as a performer because she wasn't just going to flit into big cities like a diva and simply make an appearance. Instead, Jordan's plan was to have Ashlee hit as many venues across the country as she could manage in order to prove to the world that this tomboy can really rock. "We went into this pretending that there was no TV show, no Simpson family, and no celebrity," Jordan told *Airplay Monitor.* "We've taken an old-school work ethic by bringing her to every radio station, every retailer, sometimes two states a day. She's performing acoustically everywhere she can and meeting everyone in person."

This doesn't mean that all of Ashlee's audiences were small ones. She was naturally high profile. Together with her radio interviews, she was hitting the biggest media outlets around, including launching her single, "Pieces of Me," on the popular MTV show *Total Request Live.* Although Ashlee was new to performing, she immediately had to step it up and be as good as any seasoned pro. She didn't have time to hone her skills in small, unknown clubs. "I feel like I've been thrown into the fire," she admitted to the *Monterey County Herald.* "My second show ever was performing on Jay Leno!"

The people at Geffen—particularly Jordan—really believed in her. He wouldn't have taken that grassroots approach with Ashlee and made her give it her all in tiny radio stations and in front of small crowds if he didn't have confidence in her and her music. And while there are some pop stars who need to disguise their so-so voices with crazy costumes, tons of dancers, and extreme routines to keep the audience from realizing that the star can't actually sing, Jordan wanted Ashlee to present an honest picture of who she is and how talented she is by singing her songs alone. He described his feelings about *Autobiography* to *Airplay Monitor*: "I could tell you a zillion reasons why I'm excited about this. This is one of the best records I have ever been involved with. I'm proud to have my name on it. I've worked with Limp Bizkit and Staind, and this is just as exciting to me. It's a blast to work with her, because she shines in everything she does." That's a pretty big compliment from a hard-nosed music executive!

Jordan's hunch was right, and his plan paid off. *Autobiography* sold a whopping 400,000 copies in its first week, more than doubling Jessica's best sales week ever. Almost as soon as the album went on sale, with a starting shipment of 440,000 records, reorders came pouring in. The very day *Autobiography* came out, two chain stores ordered another 150,000 records because of the white-hot demand. And when the record was featured on The Leak, an album stream on MTV.com, 2.66 million requested streams came in, which broke the previous record held by the reigning pop goddess herself, Britney Spears, for her album *In the Zone.*

The person who was most surprised by *Autobiography's* success was none other than Ashlee Simpson. She kept telling everyone that she couldn't believe the album was selling so well. She had just gone in to make a record, have some fun doing it, and hoped it would be good enough to continue with her musical career. But this was beyond her wildest dreams. (Look what happens when you set out to have a little fun!) "I had no clue that my album would do that," Ashlee said about her rocket-high record sales in the *Stratford (Ontario) Beacon Herald.* "Everything was so shocking. But it was extremely exciting. Let me tell ya, I was dancing around the room."

Autobiography entered the charts at number one in July, and by September it had gone triple platinum. In addition, Jessica's CD *In This Skin,* which had been on the charts for more than a year, hit the two million copies sold mark at about the same time. The summer of 2004 definitely belonged to the Simpson sisters. They ruled the pop charts with their genetic predisposition for stardom.

Robin Jones, vice president of programming for Radio Disney, explained why Ashlee's in-your-face persona connects with kids her age: The importance she places on being honest and truthful about her feelings and the sound she wants to produce attracts teenagers looking for the real deal. "She's not made up in her appearance, in her delivery, and obviously, in her talent," Jones said to *Airplay Monitor*. "Kids are very keen on seeing around the corner and what's real. I think that's why Ashlee has been able to reach this audience."

It was obvious that Ashlee was a fan favorite. At the 2004 Teen Choice Awards—where Lindsay Lohan, Lenny Kravitz, Paris Hilton, and loads of other celebrities gathered to receive awards voted on by thousands of teens from all over the country—Ashlee performed "Pieces of Me" and picked up not one, but two awards: Song of the Summer and Fresh Face.

And it wasn't just fans who appreciated Ashlee's album. Critics also gave her a lot of credit for putting out a solid first record. "On *Autobiography*, Ashlee proves to be a credible talent in her own right," wrote Chuck Arnold, music critic for *People* magazine. "Instead of singing the sugary pop favored by Mrs. Lachey, Ashlee brings a plucky rock edge to tunes like the crunchy 'Pieces of Me.'" While Ashlee probably didn't appreciate that dig about her sister, who wouldn't like a good review in *People*? Especially one that went on to say that Ashlee "shows promise as a composer."

Teen People's music editor Zena Burns agreed that Ashlee isn't just a one-hit wonder. Although Burns acknowledged that Ashlee had a great promotional machine and talented older sister behind her, she told *USA Today*, "[Ashlee] also came out with an insanely catchy pop single. I'm predicting she'll have the biggest pop album of the year. These days, you don't have to be the strongest, most technically gifted singer to have a hit. Ashlee's fun to watch. She wiggles her butt and clearly has a good time when she performs."

7

Reality Life

Ashlee can sing, write heartfelt and catchy songs, and wiggle her butt like a champ. That all helped her create a chart-topping album. But she made another really smart move that catapulted *Autobiography* into the stratosphere. It was something that her sister had done before her and that her father advised her to do as well, but it was also an idea she almost refused. Ashlee decided to star in her own reality show.

A lot of people want to be in reality shows—look at the craze whenever a new *American Idol* starts up or how many billionaire-

Ashlee, Nick Lachey, and Jessica at an after-party following the 2003 American Music Awards

Team Ashlee! Joe Simpson, Ashlee, and Geffen Records President Jordan Schur

Ashlee and Ryan Cabrera at the 2004 MTV Video Music Awards

Performing "Pieces of Me" at the 2004 Teen Choice Awards.

The Simpson sisters introduce Liquid Ice breath mints to the Big Apple

A still-blond Ashlee arriving at the 2004 Rock the Vote Awards

Ashlee and her band celebrating the release of her record

MTV darlings Ashlee and Jessica hanging out with Damien Fahey during *Total Request Live* at the MTV Beach House

Ashlee and Amanda Bynes having a blast at an MTV event in sunny California

wannabes stand in line to try out for Donald Trump's show, *The Apprentice*. Ashlee wasn't entirely convinced she wanted to have cameras follow her around for every second of the day. She had seen her sister go through that in *Newlyweds*, and while it had made Jessica a big star, it meant dealing with crews following you in the car, the bedroom, the kitchen, the mall . . . Ashlee wasn't sure that was her style.

Ashlee might not have been that crazy about the prospect of starring in a reality show, but her dad had his mind made up. Joe, who manages both his daughters' careers, thought the reality show would be great for Ashlee after having seen what it did for Jessica. "I decided that this was the best way to launch her as her own person," Joe told *Blender*. "It solidifies her as a person, and it also launches her as a musician and an artist."

Ashlee resisted the idea and put up a fight for a while. She wasn't wild about having cameras in her face. But her dad was persuasive—he was a preacher, after all, and a pretty smooth talker! Inevitably Ashlee's dad convinced her to go the same route as her sister, and she began filming her reality series for MTV.

The title of her show, *The Ashlee Simpson Show*, was not very creative, but the initial concept behind the program was. Each episode was to focus on one song, why Ashlee wrote it, and how it ended up sounding on the record. "Her series is *The O.C.* with music, because it's the drama of her life," Joe told *Airplay Monitor*. "It's not her being Jessica; it's her being Ashlee in her own crazy way, and it's real. It's a huge connect with kids."

The MTV executives loved that idea. "If you're a sibling of a star, you have to prove that your image is not the same as theirs," Amy Doyle, vice president of music programming for MTV, told the press. They were hoping to get two famous, and individual, Simpson stars, and the show seemed like a good way to make that happen. Plus, Ashlee had already made appearances on various shows on the network, and the executives were interested in seeing how she would break out of her sister's mold.

The Ashlee Simpson Show first aired in June 2004 and quickly became one of the top five cable shows among twelve- to thirty-four-year-old viewers. More than fifty million people tuned in to the eight-episode series to watch Ashlee get fake eyelashes glued on, flirt with her boyfriend, and go to the doctor to get her vocal cords checked. Ashlee's ratings weren't far behind her sister's wildly popular show.

As the show unfolded Ashlee progressed through the trials and tribulations of recording her first album. Viewers got to witness Ashlee lose it trying to find the right songs for her unique style, lash out at her dad, and have trouble hitting the right notes. For those interested in breaking into the music business, the show provided a real insider's view into the life of a recording artist. And not all of it was pretty. At one point Ashlee was distraught over the fact that the president of her record label didn't like her demo and wanted her to sound more like Hilary Duff. Imitating Hilary Duff was *definitely* not on Ashlee's list of things to accomplish with this record. "There are days where I would go into the studio and it sucks," she told *Airplay Monitor*. "You're not 'on' that day. There are struggles and fights, back and forth." Still, Ashlee is proud of everything she has achieved, and with good reason. It's hard work to make an album, and she couldn't wait for the MTV crowd to see it for themselves. "At the end of the day, you see the successes and what it took to get there. It's important to get yourself out there so that people know you as a person and not just the music."

Ashlee likes to differentiate between her reality program and her sister's. *The Ashlee Simpson Show* is about the process of making music, whereas singing is only one part of Jessica's show, which mainly details her life with her husband, Nick, *very* intimately. Not that Ashlee dislikes her sister's program. "I think *Newlyweds* is hysterical and I think the most amazing thing that Jessica has done for her career was *Newlyweds* because people needed to see that," she told MTV.com. "She's gorgeous, but she's normal like anybody else."

The camera crews didn't follow Ashlee around as much as they followed Jessica and Nick for *Newlyweds.* Still, they were around plenty. For about nine hours a day two days a week, Ashlee lived her life with video rolling. The whole taping process lasted approximately nine months. That might drive an ordinary person nuts, but Ashlee took it in stride. "It's cool," she said to the *Chattanooga Times Free Press* of the camera teams. "They're all like my friends now."

Of course, when cameras are following you for that long, a bunch of personal, even embarrassing moments are bound to be caught on tape. During *The Ashlee Simpson Show,* Ashlee not only launched a music career, but also moved into her own apartment (her poor mom had to visit to show her how to do laundry and clean the house). She got the heave-ho from one boyfriend, and then made her next boyfriend eat a flower to prove his love for her on Valentine's Day. Despite all the craziness that comes along with being nineteen and famous, Ashlee didn't ended up saying anything she regretted on the show, which is quite an accomplishment. She said in *YM*, "I think people expect outrageous things to come out of my mouth, but they don't."

Having been down this road before, Jessica schooled Ashlee in the ways of reality TV. Jessica told Ashlee that even though she was reluctant to put her life on display for everyone, once she decided to go ahead with the project she had to give it her all. If she acted phony in front of the cameras it would be really obvious, so she needed to relax and have fun. "She said I'd have to put it all on the table and just be myself, so that's what I've done," Ashlee told *YM*. "Having a reality show could be scary, but I don't have anything to hide."

The end result was a show that Ashlee felt fairly captured her life as it truly is. "I think it's been pretty accurate," she continued. "Those are my best friends you see me with, and that's how my life is, and that's how it is making a record. It even shows the bad days in the studio. That's why I was so happy with it, because I don't look perfect." She didn't worry about whether she would sound or look good on camera. How cool is it that Ashlee doesn't mind messing up or being goofy in front of millions of viewers? That takes a lot of confidence. "It portrayed me as me, a normal, ordinary American girl with a big nose and a big zit on her chin," she told *Blender.* "I think a lot of people will relate to me, because really, I'm just like everybody else." Yeah, right.

She is happy with how her show turned out, but Ashlee still contends that her sister is much more comfortable with living in a media fishbowl. "Jessica may be happy having cameras in her life 24/7, but not me. It's not natural; it ain't healthy," she told *Blender.* "I think a second series would drive me crazy." Meanwhile MTV reported that *The Ashlee*

Simpson Show might indeed appear for more than one season. But at the time, Ashlee defended her position. "I'm serious! This show is simply to introduce me and my album to the public," she said in *Blender.* "Once I've done that, that's it. See *ya!*" We will have to wait and see if she is able to stand up to the pressure from her dad, the MTV executives, and her thousands of fans who would love it if she let the cameras roll for another nine months.

Ashlee's dad's plan to use the show to introduce his younger daughter to the world worked. It gave Ashlee an enormous amount of exposure that most experts agree helped send *Autobiography* to the top of the charts. While her music may have garnered her a lot of fans, *The Ashlee Simpson Show* turned her into a genuine pop-culture star.

Ashlee admitted to the press that before the show, "nobody really knew that much about me. This was my way of saying, 'Here's who I am.' I chose to just be myself and let it happen and have fun." People definitely know who she is now. After the show aired, viewers knew everything from her kissing technique to her special taco recipe. It must be pretty odd to have millions of strangers know almost everything about your life, but Ashlee tries to take it in stride. "There's definitely times when I think, 'Oh my gosh, it's so weird,'" Ashlee said on *Canada AM*. Fans will come up to her and comment on her particular habits and little things usually only a good friend would know. She is flabbergasted in those moments and thinks to herself, "Wow, this person really knows me!"

Luckily, when viewers were introduced to Ashlee they really connected with her and wanted to know even more. Suddenly Ashlee was being asked to do advertisements for products such as Candies shoes and Ice Breakers Liquid Ice breath mints. Ashlee was also invited to all the hottest parties and attended major awards shows such as MTV's 2004 Video Music Awards in Miami.

Everywhere she went, photographers and reporters clamored to get a quote or picture. Everyone wanted a piece of this hot young singer!

Some experts were astounded by her meteoric rise to fame, but Ashlee understood why people found it so easy to relate to her. "Kids are a lot smarter than people sometimes think that they are," she told the *Bradenton Herald.* "More teenagers get you if you're just being yourself and being real."

8
Making Music

The good news about *Autobiography*'s success was, well, that it was so successful. Ashlee had established herself as a full-fledged musician with an exciting future in front of her. The bad news? Something would have to give. She couldn't continue acting in a major network show and singing to international audiences at the same time. So in the summer of 2004, Ashlee made a sad announcement that would disappoint millions of fans: she was leaving *7th Heaven* to dedicate herself full-time to her musical career. "Ashlee has been waiting her whole life to make this record," Jordan Schur said to *Airplay Monitor.* "She's completely focused on the music and has agreed to hold back on acting—she has turned down a number of roles so that she can develop as an artist. She has the humility and the work ethic to make this happen."

There really was no way for her to both act and sing at such a professional level. *7th Heaven* had given Ashlee her big break into show business (and her first on-screen kiss!) and she would never forget that. Some of Ashlee's happiest times happened while acting on the show, but she simply couldn't cram everything into her frantic schedule. It was too much even for a Simpson sister to handle. She was upset, but she knew she needed to follow her heart. "I'm going to miss being on set," she told *YM.* "But I've always had a passion for music and I think it's time I explored it." She discussed her decision with the show executives, and they figured out a plan. Ashlee agreed to do a few episodes to end her beloved character's story line, and then that would be it. "I love the show," she told the *Chattanooga Times Free Press*. "It really is such a great show. But with my going on tour and all that stuff, I just can't go on with it."

Once she knew she wasn't going back to *7th Heaven* and wouldn't need to look like the sweet, wholesome Cecilia, Ashlee made a characteristically bold move. She dyed her hair dark brown! Most girls would kill to have long blond hair, but not Ashlee. She loves the mysterious and punky look of her brunette locks. Some people in the media have criticized her for using her hair as a marketing ploy to distinguish herself from her sister, but Ashlee laughs off that idea, saying it's simply not true. She just loves to try new looks. Hey, you only live once!

Finally done with her commitment to *7th Heaven*, there was nothing between Ashlee and the open road. She had attracted a lot of new fans with her hit album, and it was her duty as a rocker to go out and entertain them with live gigs. When a musician hits the road, there is nothing more crucial to the tour's success than the quality of the band. And that doesn't just mean how well they play music. There are a lot of people out there who play great music, but a band also has to get along and keep each other's spirits up during long and sometimes lonely nights. Remember when Jessica was on tour and had her entire family, including Ashlee, around to keep her company? If your band isn't there for you, things can seem pretty bleak, no matter how much you rock onstage. Your band is like your family while you're on the road (that is, if you don't have your real family around like Jessica did).

Ashlee lucked out with her bandmates. She ended up with a bunch of really cool guys who also play awesome music. Ray Brady and Braxton Olita were hired to play guitar. Zach Kennedy is on bass guitar, and Chris Fox plays drums.

Braxton, Ashlee's eighteen-year-old guitarist, is originally from Hawaii. He had been in a bunch of bands before he moved to

California to attend college at the Art Institute of California–Orange County, and a hometown connection helped him land the gig with Ashlee's band. Friends from the Hawaii band National Product put Braxton in touch with Ashlee's team, he auditioned in March 2004, and soon after he was invited to join the other members of her band. They didn't have long to practice together. On June 2, 2004, they were performing on MTV's *TRL*. Braxton paid homage to his culture when he emblazoned "shaka," the Hawaiian word for "hang loose," on his guitar. "It's been just unreal in every way," Braxton said to the *Honolulu Advertiser* about becoming part of Ashlee's band. "It's a dream of just anyone who can appreciate music."

Ashlee's bandmates don't just back her up during concerts, they also keep her upbeat and down-to-earth. With all the pressure Ashlee faces every day on tour, her bandmates are there to cheer her up, support her, and sometimes cause a little harmless mayhem. "Since I always have my band with me, I'm surrounded by really fun people," Ashlee said during an MSN celebrity online chat. "At Six Flags we rode the Superman ride like six times and had so much fun. I try to surround myself with positive, happy people to keep me grounded."

Playing in front of live audiences was a new thrill for Ashlee. Sure, she had major stage fright the first time she gave it a try. But it took her only about a minute to realize that the stage is the place for her. Ashlee took to performing like a fish takes to water. "The first time I was onstage as a music artist I was very nervous," she said during the online chat. "I had my good friends with me and butterflies before I went on. But after a while I loved it. It was like nerves and then I got onstage and I was like, 'Am I really here?' Like an out-of-body experience."

Being on the road is hard. There are late nights and endless hours on the bus going from one city to the next. The equipment can malfunction. Sometimes you get a bad crowd.

Sometimes you have a bad hair day. It's like ordinary life except that you are expected to entertain night after night. Whatever challenges there may be, Ashlee says that when you get a good night with an audience that is really into the music, there is nothing better. "I think the most rewarding is playing shows now while fans are singing my songs at the top of their lungs with me," she said to MSN. "It's the coolest feeling. I always get chills. That's when everything is worth it. It's very cool."

9
On the Road

So you want to be a rock star? Who hasn't dreamed of singing to a large stadium while sitting in math class or some equally boring place? But it's not as easy as it seems. It's not all adoring fans and shopping sprees to search for cool outfits to wear onstage. There's a lot of other stuff that goes along with promoting an album and getting it out to the public. Here's a look at Ashlee's schedule in the months around her record debut. Thank goodness she is a high-energy girl.

March: Ashlee was in the recording studio

singing her heart out. She was pumped to host MTV's Spring Break Most Memorable Performances show. She probably had no idea what was in store for her as soon as she started her tour. Get some rest, Ashlee.

April: Ashlee was extremely busy putting the final touches on her album. Then she and her band got to work, practicing and perfecting their sound. Ashlee went home to L.A. for a show at the Knitting Factory late in the month. Their practicing paid off—the audience loved their performance. She and the rest of her bandmates had a great time playing for an awesome crowd, which included people of all ages.

May: Back to L.A. after traveling like a maniac to New York, Arizona, and Boston all in one week. Ashlee didn't have a minute to rest at home in California, where she appeared on *The Tonight Show* with Jay Leno. She had a blast—her very first live TV performance, and she didn't miss a single note! The next day she jammed at the Roxy. Each time she played with the band, their sound got better and better.

June 16: Ashlee's life was about to change dramatically. That night, along with millions of other viewers across America, she settled in to watch the premiere of her reality show on MTV. She hoped people liked it. They certainly did.

June 23: Ashlee logged in *a lot* of traveling time. She and the band hit four cities in only twelve hours! That's barely enough time to play a few songs, grab a cup of coffee, and get on the road again. Who said it would be easy being a rock star?

June 24: No rest for the weary. After a grueling day of travel the day before, Ashlee had to do a photo shoot for her Candies shoes ad campaign. Every girl loves shoes, but the shoot took ten hours to complete. No one likes shoes that much.

June 25: Right after a radio appearance in Detroit, Ashlee showed off her vocal cords by performing an acoustic set in Oklahoma City. She was blown away by the response. The event organizers had only planned on two hundred people showing up, but that number ended up swelling to two thousand! The sight of all those screaming fans led Ashlee to refer to the show as the "most amazing experience [she] ever had onstage" on her official Web site.

First week of July: The band hit Florida like a hurricane, visiting radio stations and playing for fans. Even though Ashlee is from Texas, she complained, "It's hot here." Texas's heat is no match for Florida's humidity. While she and the band goofed off during some free time, Ashlee found a new way to entertain herself: by making friendship bracelets. She was so into her new hobby that she made her whole band learn the craft. Figuring out how to keep herself occupied was crucial since there was a lot of waiting-around time with the band. At one show, they went on three hours late because of rain! Hobbies are a must in those situations.

July 16–July 21: The East Coast greeted Ashlee and her band. She and her boys braved the hot, sticky summer, playing awesome shows with crowds of up to seventeen thousand people. In Hartford the band got a chance to loosen up a bit while doing a show at a Six Flags amusement park. After a sound check they all jumped on the park rides. They needed to blow off steam before *Autobiography* hit stores on July 20. Ashlee and the band were on pins and needles the night before the album's debut, but the next day was incredible. In New York it was *TRL*, a Virgin Megastore album signing, and then a Geffen record release party that night. We hope Ashlee had on comfortable shoes.

July 24–July 28: Back to the West Coast. With all this zigzagging around, it's amazing the band didn't get dizzy. In Seattle, Ashlee and her band racked their brains for a band name (they had even asked fans for suggestions on her Web site). Then it was off to Orange County, where the boys from the band live. They hung out with a lot of their friends who had turned out for the local event. Ashlee took some time out from the appearance to shop for new Adidas sneakers at the mall. Later on there were more TV shows to visit—*Good Day L.A.* and *On-Air with Ryan Seacrest.* The band didn't get to chill with Ryan for long, because they had to jet to Arizona for another performance at a bowling alley, where they proved to be terrible at bowling and kept throwing gutter balls.

July 29: Ashlee finally got to go home, but not to hang out with friends, watch TV, or make tacos. She is a rock star now! This time, she was in town to do a cover shoot for *Seventeen* magazine. Ashlee certainly didn't mind; that is every teen's dream.

It was an incredibly busy summer for Ashlee, but her schedule didn't let up in the fall. When September arrived, it was time for a whole new round of television appearances and tour dates. And there was still that second season of *The Ashlee Simpson Show* to consider. . . .

10

Good Advice

Ashlee's album made ripples in the music world when it came out. Maybe more like tidal waves when you think about the huge sales figures. But one single on the CD really stood out for the tons of fans closely following the lives of both Simpson reality stars. "Shadow" raised a lot of eyebrows when it was first released, because it provides an unusual glimpse into the raw, personal thoughts of a huge star. Of course, Ashlee isn't exactly known for keeping her feelings to herself. But "Shadow" tells the tale of growing up in the background of her perfect sister's life, and the tune can be pretty harsh at certain points. As a little girl, Ashlee struggled to get any attention from her parents, who were busy helping Jessica become a star. "That song is about such an emotional feeling inside," she told the *New York Daily News*. "It's about dealing with the inner demons and the voices in your head. Around seven is when I first felt that emotional detachment about everything, and I had to overcome that."

The lyrics of "Shadow" say it all. They show Ashlee as a little girl, trying to figure out her place in this extraordinary family. She sings:

> *She was beautiful*
> *She had everything and more . . .*

"I was stuck inside someone else's life," the song continues. "And always second best."

Ashlee's life has definitely been much more dramatic than most regular people's. But dealing with an older sibling is a common occurrence (or annoyance, depending on the sibling!). Through "Shadow" Ashlee reached out to everybody who has ever had to deal with teasing, favoritism, and all that other tough family stuff. It describes the emotions that little sisters have when confronted with an older sister who always seems to get her way. "I think most siblings can relate to it," Ashlee said to *YM* about the song. "It's about finding your own identity and realizing you don't have to be like anyone else."

That's easier said than done. For a younger sister, an older sister seems to set all the rules and limits. Sure, they can also break in parents for little sisters. But when you have an older sibling like Jessica, all the expectations are set really high. Ashlee told the *New York Times,* "I was dealing with my inner demons, and my inner voices in my head. It wasn't necessarily my parents being bad parents. It was just things that I battled with in my head. Feeling second best, or feeling that they didn't love me. But the song's saying: 'Guys, I apologize, if I ever put you guys through hell. I love you, and love my life, and thank you for letting me be myself, even though I messed up at times.'"

"Shadow" is ultimately a powerful tune because it is about coming into your own. And although Ashlee apologizes to her family for messing up or hurting them, the song is decidedly unapologetic. "I had to examine my strengths and see that I was talented in my own way," she said to *YM*. "I couldn't constantly measure myself based on my sister."

You might think that her family would be angry over a song like that, but they weren't. You might also think that Ashlee would be nervous singing "Shadow" in front of her sister for the first time. But she wasn't. "I never felt weird singing in front of her," Ashlee told the *New York Post*. "When Jess first heard it, she bawled her eyes out and then told me it was the most amazing song she ever heard. She told me it was hard for her to listen to, but she's pretty proud of it, and me."

Jessica loves the entire *Autobiography* album

so much that she often listens to it before she goes onstage. She sometimes sings it in her dressing room while she is getting ready. Can you picture Jessica Simpson rocking out to "Pieces of Me" before singing a love ballad in front of thousands of fans? "She says it is the best CD she has heard this year," Ashlee told *Airplay Monitor*. "So we're very supportive of each other."

Her parents are also very supportive of Ashlee, and they understand and appreciate her music for the real place it comes from. They love "Shadow," as well as the other songs on the album, because it expresses the positive fact that their second daughter has always tried to strike out on her own. "It wasn't like I was mad at my parents or mad at my sister or anything like that," Ashlee told the *Stratford Beacon Herald*. "But it was a feeling of being the second child and saying, 'Hey, look at me, look at me! I need attention!' And I'm so not like that now. I grew out of that about four years ago."

Despite any sibling rivalry there might have

been in the past—what sisters haven't had their share of fights?—Ashlee insists that her childhood wasn't like a soap opera or a cheesy sitcom. And now that she and Jessica are adults, any hard feelings during their younger years have melted away. "People always seem to think that I struggled because I was the younger sister," she explained to *Blender*. "Sure, I wanted attention occasionally, but we were such a close family, and Jessica and I were the best of friends. Trust me, I've grown up into a well-adjusted adult."

Ashlee has stressed time and time again that she is different from her sister. Although she and Jessica are both singers now, she has done everything she can to set herself apart from her sibling. They even signed on to different record labels for that specific reason. "Once people hear my album, they'll see how different our sounds are," Ashlee told *YM*. "Being sisters is the only reason to compare us."

Still, the sisters admire each other's success. It's pretty amazing that the Simpson girls have both held top spots on the pop charts—that's definitely a cool thing to have in common. "I am so proud of Jessica," Ashlee said to *Airplay Monitor.* "She is an amazing artist with a beautiful voice. But I have never listened to the kind of music that she does. We're both doing music—but in very different ways, and it's cool."

Now that both sisters are huge stars, Jessica has again become an example for her little sister to follow. But Ashlee isn't resentful. She is happy to listen to Jessica's good sisterly advice. Having lived through a supersonic rise to the top already, Jessica can show Ashlee how to steer clear of the pitfalls of fame. And Ashlee would like to follow in her sister's footsteps when it comes to dealing with stardom. "Jessica hasn't changed a bit," she said to *YM.* "A lot of famous people lose themselves, and that's something I'll never do, because of her."

Before Ashlee entered the business, Jessica, the older and protective sister, advised her to think long and hard about jumping into the spotlight. Ashlee told *USA Today* that Jessica asked her, "'Are you sure you want to get into this?'" Ashlee, of course, decided to take the plunge despite the warning, and now that they are both pop stars, she and Jessica are closer than they have ever been. Ashlee really admires how her sister has always stayed true to herself and continues to follow her own values and ideals. "It's so good actually that we're doing the same thing because I have somebody that I can confide in and she knows," Ashlee told the *Calgary Sun*.

When Ashlee went to the Teen Choice Awards, she found out that not everyone in show business is all that nice. Now she understands why Jessica makes a quick exit from the big Hollywood events that she, as a little sister, had thought were so glamorous all those years. According to the *Calgary Sun*, on the heels of the awards show she called her big sister and said, "I see. Girls get jealous. And they're mean."

Jessica may be the big sister, but she

doesn't necessarily feel that her little sister needs much guidance anymore. "Ashlee doesn't need any advice, and Ashlee is very much an observer," Jessica said to the *Wilkes-Barre Times Leader*. "She sees decisions that I've made that are good, and decisions I've made that are bad. She's definitely well set up."

Ashlee may still seek Jessica's help from time to time, but she is definitely not taking the exact same path as her sister when it comes to relationships. That is one area where the two sisters share a very different attitude. "The guys that she would date were so different from the guys that I would date," Ashlee told *Canada AM*. "A lot of the times the younger sister is kind of more like, 'Yahoo, I want to do this and do that.'" Always the wild child!

11

Boys, Boys, Boys

Unlike her sister Jessica, who made it public that she would remain a virgin until marriage, Ashlee decided to keep her personal life, well, personal. "It's amazing that Jessica let everybody know she was a virgin, and it changed a lot of people's lives," she told *YM*. "I decided that I didn't want to talk about that because it is super personal."

Jessica talked incessantly about her dreams of a wedding day, and when she finally did get hitched to Nick, their fairy-tale wedding was captured on television during an *InStyle* wedding special. From Jessica's wedding dress to the flowers, everything was perfect (of course it was, this is Jessica we're talking about!). Ashlee certainly didn't spend her childhood lying on her bed, daydreaming about a future with Prince Charming. She was too busy playing air guitar to Joan Jett! Ashlee wants to take it slow when it comes to that kind of lifelong commitment. She told *YM,* "I've got a few more life lessons to learn before I get married."

It's a good thing that Ashlee has that kind of attitude, because she is definitely learning a lot of lessons when it comes to boys. So far she hasn't gone for the solid kind of guy that Jessica chose. On the contrary, she has made more adventurous choices, picking boyfriends who might be a lot of fun, but also a lot of trouble.

Case in point was Ashlee's first serious boyfriend—the detached and too-cool-for-school Josh Henderson. Every girl gets her heart broken, even Ashlee Simpson. But the first time is always incredibly painful (not that it's ever easy). Josh was the first important boy in her life, or as Ashlee described it to *Entertainment Weekly*, he was her "first heart-break, first love, and like, all that stuff."

Born in Tulsa, Oklahoma, on October 25, 1981, Josh was a jock, playing center field for the Tulsa Memorial High School baseball team. After high school he moved to Dallas and worked as a dancing waiter at a Joe's Crab Shack.

Josh wasn't dancing crab claws out to hungry customers for long. In 2001 he was chosen to be a cast member of the television show *Popstars 2*. The WB program followed Josh and the four other members of his TV-fabricated band, Scene 23. The band lived in a five-story house in West Hollywood, California, put together an album, and learned how to perform. Even though he had never sung in public before, Josh beat out more than eight thousand other people who auditioned to get a spot on the show by wowing the judges with his rendition of the *NSYNC song "Bye, Bye, Bye"

Despite his innate talent, Josh nearly didn't

get the part, because he was goofing around at the auditions. Just before his dance audition, he tried to jump up and touch a chandelier at the hotel where the contest was being held. He fell on his ankle, tore a tendon, and was rushed to the hospital. Josh thought his chance to make it on a major television show had gone down the drain. But the judges liked him so much, they told him that if he could make it to the Miami auditions several weeks away (which included paying his own way), they would give him another shot. Josh threw himself into his physical therapy, and in Miami he danced his way to the next round of auditions and eventually onto the show.

After *Popstars 2* aired, Josh landed a starring role in a sitcom on Fox. The show, called *Newton,* was about a perfect American town where there is one of every different type of person, and Josh's character comes to threaten the town's harmony. Sounds like a perfect role for Josh, but *Newton* never made it past the first episode and failed to become a TV series.

Ashlee and Josh managed to keep their two-year relationship under the radar. That is, until they broke up! They split up in front of millions of people on the first episode of *The Ashlee Simpson Show*. Ashlee said during an MSN online chat, "I looked at love differently and we can all look back on love and smile and be happy because that's life." And while getting dumped is no fun, there is one good thing to come out of heartbreak (at least for Ashlee): It provides really good material for writing songs.

Her split with Josh gave Ashlee a lot of inspiration for the songs on her album. In fact, it seems like many of the lyrics on her first CD are about him. "The breakup left me with a painful, empty feeling," she described to *YM*. "I was like, 'Oh, no, my life is over.' But then you see that boys aren't everything."

Those who tuned in to *The Ashlee Simpson Show* got to watch the ups, downs, and eventual end of her relationship with Josh. While a lot of people would be horrified to see themselves with an old flame messing around on a reality TV show, Ashlee doesn't mind. "It's actually good for me to see that now and say: 'Oh, that's why I'm not with him. Because he's a jerk,'" she told *USA Today.*

Ashlee never regretted that Josh became a thing of the past. After their breakup, they saw each other at an L.A. club where he basically ignored her. That really made her angry, and you don't want to get on Ashlee's bad side. "I know this is really dorky," she told *Entertainment Weekly*, "But when he was leaving I stood and flipped him off. I was really mad. Really mad." Josh was acting as if he hardly knew her, let alone kissed her on national TV. That's pretty lame.

Although she had just suffered her first broken heart, Ashlee moved on like a true tough chick. Her family, of course, was a big help. When it comes to boys, Ashlee relies on her brother-in-law, Nick, for the serious advice. "Every time I have boyfriend trouble, he gives me the right answer: 'Make the guy jealous,'" she told *People.* Ashlee couldn't wait until Josh heard her album. She knew that would be the best revenge!

"Guys come and go," she said to *Entertainment Weekly.* "But you're the one that has to stay strong." Ashlee followed her own advice and got over Josh in a flash. Her recovery period was so quick that she started dating her next cutie, musician Ryan Cabrera, while still filming *The Ashlee Simpson Show.*

In December 2003 Ashlee made a steamy guest appearance in Ryan's music video for his song "On the Way Down." When the filming began, Ashlee didn't hold anything back. "I totally pulled him against the wall and started making out with him," she told *Teen People.* For his part, Ryan, who is two years older than Ashlee, told the magazine, "That was crazy—I was shocked." Oh how cute, Ryan's shy. Well not that shy . . .

Even more shocking than their make-out scene in the video was when Ashlee and Ryan surprised everyone by becoming a couple, since Ryan had been a longtime family friend. Ashlee can't seem to get enough of those Texas men—like Josh, Ryan also lived in the Lone Star State before moving to L.A. Besides being cute and talented, Ryan had something else going for him when it came to winning Ashlee's heart: He really clicked with her family. With the Simpsons that isn't as easy as throwing a football around with her dad or helping her mom out around the house. This is a professional family. But Ryan has his own musical aspirations, and was like the sixth member of the Simpson clan (the fifth being Nick, of course!). Not only did Ashlee's dad, Joe, manage Ryan, just like he does for Ashlee and her sister, but also Ryan was the opening act for Jessica's tour. What a way to promote his album!

Ryan and Ashlee's love affair was a big part of her reality TV show. Once the program aired on MTV, their relationship was thrust into the spotlight. The couple was featured on TV and in popular magazines such as *Us*

Weekly, to which Ashlee described Ryan as "my best friend in the whole world."

Ashlee and Ryan shared an important bond when it came to their music. They had similar views on the craft. They both believed strongly that you have to play, play, play in order to sound good and become a real performer. "I've played in bars to no one but the bartender," Ryan told the *Vancouver Province*. "If you can play in front of nobody, you can play in front of thousands." Ryan wanted to play so badly for audiences that he would go to sorority houses where he didn't know anybody, knock on the door, and ask the unsuspecting sorority sister who answered if he could play for the girls. Most of them let him. Who wouldn't let that cutie on the doorstep come in and strum a couple of tunes on his guitar?

When it came to musical influences, Ashlee and Ryan had very different sources. She liked the hard-rocking ladies of the eighties. He preferred more mellow fare, such as the Beatles and Paul Simon. Ryan loves watching the transformation in his audiences as he plays, getting people to go from skeptical to downright rockin' out. He is confident about his first album, *Take It All Away,* and says that every song on the record holds its own. "I'm like a goofy kid. I wanted to make a positive album that made people feel good," he said to the *Vancouver Province.* "At the same time, I have a darker, more quirky side. So I tried to make a record that was a balance. I tried to touch on all the emotions." No wonder he and Ashlee ended up together! They could seriously relate to each other's quirky personalities.

Ashlee gave Ryan the biggest tribute any girlfriend could give a guy: She wrote "Pieces of Me," the hit song that launched her career, about *him.* "I wrote about just like the whole time I was doing my record," Ashlee told *Canada AM.* "He was, like, there for me."

Ashlee and Ryan had a blast together. They loved to go out and spend time with each other doing fun, everyday things. On one date, they went on a shopping spree where Ryan had to buy Ashlee her sister's album *In This Skin* because she didn't even own it yet. Can you believe it? Then they indulged their love for vintage clothes by going scavenging for old T-shirts and picking out a couple for a dollar. After working up an appetite shopping, they gorged themselves on mozzarella sticks and other fried foods. That doesn't seem like a typical date for two hot pop stars, does it? Au contraire, these two loved a nice down-home evening. "We like to have taco-offs to see who can cook better tacos," Ryan told *Teen People*. Ashlee agreed that her favorite dates were the ones where the two drove around listening to music, had a low-key dinner, and then went home to watch a movie. "I'm a chill person. I don't like when people go to extremes to try to impress me," she told *YM*. "It's awkward when someone really tries. I'm just always myself, so I want a guy who's the same."

Ashlee is confident about herself and who she is. That didn't change when she got a boyfriend. Some girls will try to alter their look so that they can please their boyfriends' tastes. But not Ashlee. She doesn't get all dolled up for a guy, and she certainly doesn't care what her boyfriends have to say about her style. Ryan told *Teen People* about what would happen if he commented on Ashlee's jeans: "Even if I said her butt looked horrible she'd say, 'I don't care—I like it!'"

It might seem like a lot of fun to be a cool and confident rock star dating another cool and confident rock star, but there is definitely a downside. Ashlee's and Ryan's careers were so demanding that it proved difficult to have a regular relationship. In August 2004 Ashlee and Ryan split. The official reason was that they broke up because of conflicting work schedules (don't stars always say that?), while friends said that each of the singers was so occupied with touring and promoting their individual albums that they didn't have time for each other. After consulting their schedules, they realized it would be about a year before they would have time to see each other.

August was definitely a crazy month for both Ashlee and Ryan. While Ashlee was hitting the top spots on the pop charts, Ryan wasn't doing so badly himself. As a newcomer, his single "On the Way Down" ranked in the top five of *TRL*'s hit list. *Take It All Away* was released on August 17 and hit the number eight spot when it debuted on the Billboard 200. Like Ashlee, Ryan had a hectic round of publicity events to kick off the album, which included album signings at Rockefeller Center, performances on *TRL* and *Good Morning America,* in-store appearances at Tower Records, and about a million other meet-and-greet events. Ryan had worked hard on that album—he had teamed up with John Rzeznik of the Goo Goo Dolls, who had pushed the young performer to give it his all when it came to his music—and he wanted to do anything to get it out to the public.

Ryan owes part of the excitement over his album to Ashlee and her reality TV show, where he made many appearances that allowed thousands of fans to get to know him long before they knew his music. But Ryan hopes that his music will keep him in the public eye long after his reality TV show appearances have ended. "I don't want to be something that just comes in and goes out," he told MTV.com. "I want people to see that I can actually play, and I want to do this forever, not just have a couple records."

Their breakup was very abrupt and startled a lot of fans. Ashlee and Ryan had seemed like a great couple, and they had always been really close. Maybe no one was more surprised about the split than Ashlee. "Ryan's my best friend, and he's the only one who gets me," she told *YM*. "After a long day, he'll come over and I forget about everything else." Love is a hard thing to predict, and as Ashlee noted herself, she still has a lot of lessons to learn.

12

Family Ties

The Simpsons are a remarkable family. How many households are you aware of where the parents are savvy record-industry pros and both daughers are superstars? There have been plenty of opportunities for Jessica, and now Ashlee, to become spoiled. The girls can buy anything they want (and Jessica often does, much to Nick's dismay). Still, by all accounts, they aren't brats. They are the same level-headed girls they were when they were growing up in Texas. The Simpsons all say that success hasn't changed their family much. They get along well, they are very protective of one another, and they are wary of anyone other than their closest friends. Just about the only thing that has changed is Joe's vocabulary. Now that he is a music manager and no longer a preacher, he sometimes uses colorful language—like the record execs he deals with—to make a point.

Despite any new words he has picked up in L.A., Joe is still the more rational, authoritative parent. Tina is definitely the softy. She may seem pretty conventional at times, but Tina is not a typical mom. In fact, she has always been accepting of her younger daughter's offbeat ways. Tina described her attitude toward Ashlee to *Blender*: "If she wanted to show up in church in the shortest skirt imaginable—as long as it wasn't indecent, of course—then good for her. I didn't care if she wanted to go to Mass in nothing but a pair of boots and a leotard. I always encouraged self-expression."

Ashlee took her mom's encouragement and ran with it. Tina's advice and support has allowed Ashlee to be truly independent. That is part of the reason she doesn't feel threatened by all of Jessica's accomplishments. She sees her own achievements and those of her sister as all part of the same big effort. "For us it's not about competition," she told an AP reporter. "If she succeeds, then I'm happy, and if I succeed, then our family wins no matter what."

Tina tried to teach her daughters that being themselves is more important than being beautiful or being a great dancer or singer. "And if you want to know why both my daughters are so well-adjusted, it's because I've always taught them to know exactly who they are, to be happy with who they are and to stay that way," Tina said to *Blender*. Having a cool mom like that is obviously helpful in becoming a confident, self-assured individual. Ashlee and Jessica both realize that and are best friends with their mom (they still fight for her attention!).

The three Simpson ladies are such good

friends that Tina and Ashlee were the ones who organized Jessica's bachelorette party, which took place two days before she married Nick. And this wasn't any kind of prim and proper tea party. Ashlee and Tina held the party for fifty female guests at the Whiskey Bar in Austin, Texas where female belly dancers and cute male dancers provided the entertainment. Tina isn't too old to have fun with her daughters—not by a long shot!

Tina has been incredibly supportive of all Ashlee's endeavors, especially her music. "My mom loves rock," Ashlee told the *New York Times*. "She jams to my CD. It's so cute." That doesn't mean Tina shares all her daughter's tastes, however. They have those typical mother-daughter moments in the car when Tina has to turn down the radio before she has a heart attack or car crash because Ashlee is blaring her favorite rock band at full volume. Ashlee laughs it off because she knows her mom is trying as hard as she can to relate. "My mom had rock living in her, so now I kind of got to open her up to it," she said.

All the Simpsons are close, but Ashlee and her mom have a special connection. "My mom is incredible. I always listen to her," Ashlee told the *New York Times*. "We're best friends and at the same time we'll butt heads every now and then because we have the exact same personality." Like Ashlee, Tina is the younger of two sisters and was the out-of-control sibling at times. Or, as Ashlee described, "She was the crazy one—not the party-crazy one, just the crazy one."

That may explain why, when Ashlee made the bold move to dye her hair brown, her mother was with her all the way. "When I came up from the sink, I was incredibly shocked," Ashlee told the *New York Times*. "My mom loved it." Joe is much more traditional, but eventually he came around to the dark hair also. Ashlee proclaimed, "My dad, who loves blond long hair, likes it brown better now too."

It's been more difficult for Joe to come

around to other lifestyle changes that go along with having two pop stars in the family. Surrounded by three spontaneous, impulsive women, it's not surprising that Joe is often the strict voice of authority. Which makes sense—he was a minister, right? But despite the fact that Joe was a preacher, his family insists he wasn't the square, stern kind. "My dad was a real cool, hip youth minister," Jessica told the *Dallas Morning News*. "It wasn't like church was ever boring for us. . . . Dad always made it interesting and fun. We'd have church around the pool on Sunday nights."

Joe made Christianity seem cool, because he wanted to appeal to kids who normally wouldn't set foot inside a church, or to those who were into their faith but didn't want to seem like they were geeks who would rather sit around studying the Bible than go to the mall. Maybe it was this ability to know what kids like and how to relate to them that helped him launch his daughters' careers. Joe sacrificed a lot, both in time and money, to get Jessica started singing professionally. Later he advised Ashlee in the business. Through both of his daughters, Joe has developed a mini show business empire.

Joe Simpson is not the first father to have children who become famous siblings. There are many stories of younger sisters and brothers who have gotten into their older sibling's act. "You have young girls like Jessica Simpson and Britney Spears and Hilary Duff making such a great living," Atoosa Rubenstein, editor of *Seventeen* magazine, told the *New York Daily News*. "If you have another daughter or son who is equally talented, why wouldn't you want them in the family business?" Joe manages both his daughters in what can be an incredibly difficult industry, and he has learned a lot since his early days of leading Jessica around the Christian music circuit. Now he goes head-to-head with the biggest record labels in the country. "My dad has become this incredible manager," Ashlee said to the *New York Times*. "People really, truly respect him now. And it took him a while to gain that respect in this industry." In fact, Joe is so highly respected, he recently signed a management deal with Geffen Records!

It's understandable that curse words have become part of Ashlee's dad's transformation. He has had to become tougher in some ways now that he is a full-fledged member of the music business, but he can also relax a bit more than during his days as a preacher. When he first heard Ashlee's song "La La," which is a sassy song about sex, Ashlee told the *New York Post,* "His jaw hit the floor. He didn't know what to say." But she added that after he listened to it again, he said to her, "'You know what? This one's gonna be a hit. I love it. It's a good song.'" Despite his personal feelings toward his daughter and how he thinks she should behave, Joe was able to separate his roles as Ashlee's father and manager.

Ashlee's relationship with Joe, whether as her manager or her dad, isn't always smooth. They can get into some pretty big disagreements (as viewers of *The Ashlee Simpson Show* have witnessed). Ashlee is not the perfect little daddy's girl that Jessica appears to be. "My dad and I, we'll like go head-to-head and fight," she told MTV.com. "I have to admit it, and sometimes I don't want to, but . . . me and my dad are very strong-minded and what we say is how we feel and we're not going left or right of it." Still, they don't let hard feelings linger too long. Immediately after they fight, Ashlee will usually apologize and tell her father that she's sorry and she loves him. "Because we love each other at the end of the day, and I know even if I want to fight him for something, I know that he's not out to get me."

Fights or no fights, Joe is bursting with pride over the success of his children. They are living out dreams he was never able to achieve himself. "I used to want to be an actor when I was young," he told *Blender*. "But my family was real poor, so that was never a realistic possibility for me. But now I'm happy living vicariously through my children. See, I'm a creative person, and this is my way of doing what I was born to do—be creative. That's my gift to my girls."

Ashlee knows she is lucky to have such a loving, supportive family behind her. While a lot of teenagers think it's very uncool to hang out with their families, Ashlee disagrees. "People are always like, 'Oh, it's very weird that your parents hang out with you,'" she remarked. "But it's not. It's so great. I don't hide one thing from my parents."

13
Great Expectations

There's no denying that Ashlee is an international superstar. But that doesn't mean her idea of a good time is driving in limos, wearing evening gowns, or attending fancy awards ceremonies. She's actually pretty much an average nineteen-year-old girl. "I love to be a dork with my friends and have fun. I'm not taking things so seriously," she told *USA Today*. For her, being a dork includes her favorite hobbies, which are cooking and painting lamps. She loves to hang out at her L.A. apartment—which is always a mess—with Lauren Zelman, her roommate and best friend from elementary school. Days off are rare for the young star, but when she gets one, a perfect afternoon is out of the limelight, hanging with her girlfriends, doing nothing except eating popcorn and watching movies.

In the months to come it might get much more difficult for Ashlee to stay out of the spotlight. Even people who always believed she would be a success have been amazed at just how far Ashlee has come in such a short amount of time. Her very first album hit number one on the charts, and that is just the beginning. Music industry experts and executives see a long future in store for Ashlee. Evan Harrison, AOL Music vice president and general manager told *Airplay Monitor,* "To be nineteen and showing the signs she is already, promises a bright future. She's going to have long legs and take people by surprise. We see a big run ahead for Ashlee." In an industry filled with one-hit wonders, that is a huge compliment.

The odds of Ashlee being a one-hit wonder

are slim. Music is in Ashlee's blood and has always been a family activity. Since Jessica, Ashlee, and their mom love to sit around and sing together, it seems like a natural evolution for the sisters to perform as a duo now that they are both bona fide professional musicians. But those clamoring to buy a ticket to the Simpson Family Reunion tour will just have to wait. The sisters say they don't have any plans to hit the road together anytime soon. For now Ashlee is happy to tour with her own band and continue working on her solo career. That doesn't mean she has ruled out duets with Jess. One day she would like to sing onstage with her sister. She envisions them collaborating on something totally different from both of their typical styles, such as singing the blues. And Ashlee will sing with Jessica on her big sister's upcoming Christmas album. Whatever the girls do in the future, one thing is for sure: They will have a sold-out audience.

Now that Ashlee Simpson has become a

household name, the younger Simpson sister is learning that a lot of pressure comes with being a celebrity. Famous people are constantly under scrutiny by the press. Plus, because of her high record sales, Ashlee is expected to keep putting out hits. All this could really get to a girl, especially one who didn't get to do the normal things most teens do. Even her sister got to go to the prom, but Ashlee, who finished school at sixteen, missed out on all of those typical high school experiences that most teenagers go through and learn from. Still, Ashlee insists she is content with all the choices she has made during her nineteen years. "I have a great life," she said to the *Monterey County Herald.* "If I had to go back, I wouldn't change a thing."

If anything, Ashlee is looking for opportunities to put even more pressure on herself. She would like to branch out into other cool ventures and has expressed interest in creating her own clothing line. "I love clothes and I've always wanted to do my own thing," she said during an MSN celebrity online chat. "I would love to have a young, funky, more laid-back kind of Marc Jacobs [clothing line]."

And although she left *7th Heaven* to pursue singing, Ashlee is also interested in returning to acting. Directors and producers eager to put her on their lists of hot, talented young actresses have been sending her scripts, which she has been reading to see if there is a part that would be suitable for her, and in September 2004 Ashlee signed on as part of the cast of the upcoming film *Wannabe*. Ashlee will play an actor in the movie, which is about a musician who quits his singing career to pursue acting. The film is scheduled to release in 2005.

One thing that Ashlee is not planning to do in the future is appear naked in films or photos. It is important to her family that she doesn't engage in what they consider to be inappropriate behavior. That doesn't mean she isn't confident about her body; she's just not about to flaunt it like that. "I know exactly what's under this T-shirt," she told *Blender*. "But I'm going to keep it under wraps."

Despite all her side projects, music fans needn't worry. Ashlee isn't giving up her rock career anytime soon. She continues to pursue her passion for self-expression through music, even with her busy schedule of touring and making public appearances. "Every time I get a second to be alone, I always write," she said during an MSN online chat. "Making an album is fun. I am definitely still writing."

Ashlee sincerely hopes to remain a central figure in the music business. As she told *Canada AM,* "I love doing what I do. It's fun." But there are other things in life besides work, and Ashlee has dreams beyond the various facets of her career. Even though she is a bit of a rebel and probably still has a lot of boyfriends in her future, Ashlee would like to settle down and get married one day. She just has no idea when. "Eventually I want to do that—to get married," she told the *New York Times.* She also dreams of having a house in

Austin, a ranch with its own recording studio, and a husband at her side to enjoy it all with her. But those days are far into the future. "That whole world would be great. But you know, you never know where life will take you."

14
Fun Fast Facts

1. Name: Ashlee Simpson

2. Birthday: October 3, 1984

3. Birthplace: Dallas, Texas

4. Current home: Los Angeles, California

5. Zodiac sign: Libra

6. Parents: Joe and Tina Simpson

7: Siblings: older sister Jessica (as if you didn't know that)

8. Favorite movie: *True Romance.* "It's violent but the love story is good. I'm an old-school movie lover," Ashlee said during an MSN online chat.

9. Favorite weather: Rainy days, because she loves to frolic in puddles, getting soaking wet.

10. Celebrity crush: Maroon 5's drummer, Ryan Dusick.

11. How Ashlee keeps up her energy: She downs the highly caffeinated soft drink Red Bull. "I can't live without it," she said to *Teen People.* "I drink three or four every day."

12. Ashlee has a serious sweet tooth. She can't get enough of candy like Laffy Taffys and Nerds.

13. Favorite chore: doing laundry. Ashlee actually enjoys washing her duds. "I think it's fun. There is nothing better than clean

clothes," she said during an interview on the Web site ign.com.

14. Favorite TV channel: The Discovery Channel. Ashlee loves science!

15. Favorite make-out song: Maroon 5's "Secret." Ashlee said, "I advise anybody who's going to be kissing to put that song on."

15

Ashlee's Style Guide

Be True to Yourself

That's Ashlee's motto for everything she does. Discussing her style, she told *USA Today*, "I am a tomboy with a girly twist." She doesn't see any problem with wearing ladylike Chanel sunglasses, a frilly shirt, and a stack of jelly bracelets that first became cool when Madonna was climbing the charts in the eighties. Ashlee doesn't worry if things aren't on the latest cover of *Vogue* or if they don't technically "go" together. If she likes it, she puts it on.

TIP: No matter what fads or styles are popular, go with what you like. Don't follow the cool girls. Be your own leader.

Be Adventurous

The day Ashlee left the WB show *7th Heaven,* she commemorated her career change by dying her hair dark brown. It was a radical move for someone about to launch a record career. Don't they say that blondes have more fun? Ashlee didn't think so. She said of her new hair color, "I love it. I think it makes me look older," she told an AP reporter.

TIP: Make a style change to mark a new period of your life. Wear your hair in a new way for the first day of school, or after meeting a new guy, try a lipstick that you never thought you would wear. It'll keep people guessing about the next trick you have up your sleeve.

Do Try Smoky Eyes

There isn't a picture of Ashlee where her light-colored eyes don't pop out from her milky white skin and mane of dark hair. That's because she loves to work that gorgeous smoky look around her eyes. Whether it's full-on black eyeliner, like she wore for her "Shadow" video, or just a little bit of blue color smudged around the edges, the result is glamorous.

TIP: After putting on liner or shadow, apply two coats of a volume or plumping mascara. Wiggle the brush around while applying to get as much mascara as you can on your lashes. Then bat away.

Don't Match

"I tend to put a lot of random things together, ever since I was a little kid," Ashlee said in the *New York Times*. Her outfits could be as random as cowboy boots and a leotard or snow boots with tights, but somehow it always looks awesome all together, doesn't it? We can't all have the eye for style (or the massive closet of clothes) that Ashlee does, but once in a while it's fun to shake it up and ditch the typical jeans and T-shirt uniform.

TIP: Loosen up. It's okay if your socks don't match your shirt. Try wearing an outfit where everything isn't so predictable. Put a vintage slip over some old jeans for a romantic bohemian look, or wear your oldest pair of sneakers with a cute party dress for an effortless appearance and a painless night of dancing.

OKAY, SOMETIMES IT'S FINE TO MATCH . . . AND LISTEN TO YOUR MOM

Ashlee's outlandish getups can be a little too, well, outlandish. Luckily she has her mom around to rein it in, and to pull together an outfit with some matching shoes, so that onstage Ashlee will look like a star and not a crazy person. "She'll make sense of something," Ashlee said in the *New York Times*. "And keep it my style, but make it more TV-friendly."

TIP: Have someone around whom you can trust to make sure your experimental style doesn't go haywire.

Don't Be Afriad to Tear it Up

Everyone knows Ashlee likes to look like a rocker chick. So sometimes she'll rip up her shirts, which definitely gives a tough edge to her sweet smile and pretty features.

TIP: Rip up a few old tanks and continue to wear those old jeans with the hole in the knee. But make sure you don't rip up anything you've borrowed from a good friend. . . .

Definitely Don't Sacrifice Comfort for Fashion

"I like to be comfortable," Ashlee said in *Teen People*. "I'm very laid back." That translates into fitted T-shirts, denim skirts, and of course sneakers, all of which are staples of Ashlee's wardrobe.

TIP: No matter how pretty the shoes are, if they are too tight, don't wear them. It's not worth the pain. The same goes for tight pants or any clothes with too many buckles or zippers. There are so many clothes out there that are cute and comfy. Why torture yourself?

There's No Such Thing as Too Many T-shirts

Ashlee is crazy for all kinds of T-shirts, but especially vintage ones. They are unique, and already soft from years of someone else washing them! Her ex Ryan Cabrera once teased Ashlee that she had more old T-shirts than a secondhand store.

TIP: Peruse your local vintage stores for great T-shirts with funny logos. It doesn't matter if you have no idea what the slogans and pictures mean, because you can just make it up. They are more interesting than anything you can find at the mall, and cheaper too!

Keep Your Skin Clean

With all the heavy makeup Ashlee has to wear while she is performing or being photographed for magazines, her skin definitely needs some TLC. She relies on Cetaphil, a mild face wash, to clear it up immediately. The over-the-counter cleanser is perfect for Ashlee's skin, which is very sensitive and gets easily irritated by harsh detergents.

TIP: Wash your face every morning and night with a mild face wash that doesn't dry out your skin.

Shop Around

Ashlee doesn't limit herself to one store or brand. From Urban Outfitters to Marc Jacobs to local vintage stores, Ashlee picks her duds from a wide variety of places. It's easier that way for her to mix and match her wardrobe, and she doesn't end up looking like a walking advertisement for a designer.

TIP: Don't just head to the trendy store in town when you go shopping. Have fun with changing styles, and also keep an open mind about stores you normally wouldn't visit.

There might be a cute top lurking in that old-granny store. No one else at school will have it, that's for sure!

Will You Regret It?

At one point Ashlee wanted to get a star tattoo on her foot, but Jessica somehow knew that was not the right decision for her little sister. So big sis came home with a present for Ashlee: a key chain with a star on it from Tiffany & Co. Ashlee told *People* that Jessica said to her, "'I'm giving you this so you don't get that tattoo.'"

TIP: To be fashionable you have to take some risks, but be careful of taking things too far. If you have an urge to do something really crazy with your look, maybe you should sleep on it and consult good friends and family members. If you plan any permanent changes, try to imagine if you'll like it when you are sixty!

16

Past, Present, and Future

ASHLEE'S CAREER TIMELINE

1998 *Total Request Live* . . . Ashlee appears on the popular MTV video countdown show. (Who knew back then that Ashlee would return to the show six years later as a singing sensation?)

2001 *Malcolm in the Middle* . . . Ashlee appears as a high school student.

2002 Ashlee is a dancer on Jessica's Dreamchaser Tour.

2002 *The Hot Chick* . . . Monique

2002 *Seventh Heaven* . . . Cecilia Smith

2002 Ashlee records "Just Let Me Cry" for the *Freaky Friday* soundtrack.

2003 Ashlee appears on *Newlyweds: Nick & Jessica,* giving the audience a taste of what's to come.

2004 *The Ashlee Simpson Show*

2004 Nickelodeon Teen Choice Awards: Ashlee performs and picks up two awards!

2004 Ashlee co-hosts the MTV Movie Awards Preshow.

Coming Up:

2005 *Wannabe* . . . Ashlee will play a singer in this upcoming film—what a stretch!

Web site-ings

As we've learned, the Simpson sisters are always on the go. They're either trying something different, signing on to new projects, or showing off a new talent their fans didn't know existed. After a whirlwind year in 2004, you'd think that Ashlee would consider taking some time off. But this girl just doesn't quit! If you're interested in learning what Ashlee's up to, you can go online to the following Web sites and catch up on the latest Simpson scoop:

Ashlee's Official Web Site
www.ashleesimpsonmusic.com

The Official Ashlee Simpson Fan Site
www.ashleesimpson.net

Internet Movie Database
http://us.imdb.com/name/nm1249883

TV Tome
http://www.tvtome.com/tvtome/servlet/PersonDetail/personid-23236

Ashlee Simpson Fan
http://www.fan-sites.org/ashlee-simpson

Eonline—facts, credits, and news stories
http://www.eonline.com/Facts/People/Bio/0,128,72570,00.html